"Let's go, Goldie," said Annie. "Mom needs us to get some birthday candles for your cake."

As soon as Goldie and Annie left, their mom and dad hid the clues for a treasure hunt.

When Goldie and Annie came back with the candles, their mom said, "Goldie, it is time for your birthday treasure hunt."

Their dad said, "There
is a surprise for you
at the end. Just follow
the clues. Here is the
first clue."

Goldie unfolded the
clue. It said, "Walk
past the TV and look
under the goldfish bowl."

Goldie followed the first clue and found a new folded clue under the goldfish bowl.

The clue said, "Turn
and face the plates in
the case. Look next to
them in the yellow vase."

Goldie went right to
the case. She reached
in the vase and found
the next clue.

It said, "Go to the
kitchen. Look for your
school folder. The clue
is nearby, under the
potholder."

In the kitchen, Goldie
picked up the last clue.

It said, "Soon you will
get your big surprise.
Now use this scarf
to cover your eyes."

Goldie's dad helped
her tie the scarf. Then
Annie took her hand.

Annie led Goldie to
the playroom. Goldie
started to giggle.

"Now take off the scarf,
Goldie," said Annie,
"and step inside for
your big surprise!"

"Surprise!" yelled all
of Goldie's friends.
"You are right," Goldie
said to her mom and
dad. "My friends are
a treasure!"

15

When her mom and dad
came in with the cake,
her friends sang "Happy
Birthday." The candles
flickered with a golden glow
until Goldie blew them out.